Lexile: _3 2 0 L_

AR/BL: _2.0_

AR Points: _0.5_

HOSPITAL HELPER

Written by Joanne Meier and Cecilia Minden • Illustrated by Bob Ostrom
Created by Herbie J. Thorpe

ABOUT THE AUTHORS

Joanne Meier, PhD, has worked as an elementary school teacher, university professor, and researcher. She earned her BA in early childhood education from the University of South Carolina, and her MEd and PhD in education from the University of Virginia. She currently works as a literacy consultant for schools and private organizations. Joanne lives in Virginia with her husband Eric, daughters Kella and Erin, two cats, and a gerbil.

Cecilia Minden, PhD, is the former director of the Language and Literacy Program at the Harvard Graduate School of Education. She is now a reading consultant for school and library publications. She earned her PhD in reading education from the University of Virginia. Cecilia and her husband, Dave Cupp, live outside Chapel Hill, North Carolina. They enjoy sharing their love of reading with their grandchildren, Chelsea and Qadir.

ABOUT THE ILLUSTRATOR

Bob Ostrom has been illustrating children's books for nearly twenty years. A graduate of the New England School of Art & Design at Suffolk University, Bob has worked for such companies as Disney, Nickelodeon, and Cartoon Network. He lives in North Carolina with his wife Melissa and three children, Will, Charlie, and Mae.

ABOUT THE SERIES CREATOR

Herbie J. Thorpe had long envisioned a beginning-readers' series about a fun, energetic bear with a big imagination. Herbie is a book lover and an avid supporter of libraries and the role they play in fostering the love of reading. He consults with librarians and matches them with the perfect books for their students and patrons. He lives in Louisiana with his wife Misty and their daughter Carson.

The Child's World®

Published in the United States of America by The Child's World®
1980 Lookout Drive • Mankato, MN 56003-1705
800-599-READ • www.childsworld.com

Acknowledgments
The Child's World®: Mary Berendes, Publishing Director
The Design Lab: Kathleen Petelinsek, Design;
Kari Tobin, Page Production
Artistic Assistant: Richard Carbajal

Library of Congress Cataloging-in-Publication Data
Meier, Joanne D.
  Hospital helper / by Joanne Meier and Cecilia Minden ;
illustrated by Bob Ostrom.
     p. cm. — (Herbster readers)
  ISBN 978-1-60253-218-2 (library bound : alk. paper)
  [1. Hospitals—Fiction. 2. Voluntarism—Fiction. 3. Bears—
Fiction.] I. Minden, Cecilia. II. Ostrom, Bob, ill. III. Title.
IV. Series.

PZ7.M5148Hos 2009
[E]—dc22   2009003995

Grandma Bear goes to the hospital every Wednesday morning. But she is not sick!

3

Grandma Bear is a volunteer. She visits patients staying in the hospital. She delivers flowers and mail.

Grandma Bear has been a volunteer for a long time. She knows almost everyone! People are always happy to see her.

On this morning, Herbie had come along to help volunteer. He was nervous. He was worried that he might get in the way.

"Are you sure I can help?" asked Herbie. He wondered what he would say to the patients.

"You'll be great," said Grandma.

11

The doctors and nurses were very friendly.
"Nice to see you, Herbie!" said Dr. Reed.

"We're so glad you're here!" said Nurse Brown.

"Today we will deliver flowers," said Grandma. "It's one of my favorite jobs! Just look at this beautiful cart."

Grandma and Herbie got on the elevator.
Herbie pushed the button for the third floor.

When the doors opened, they carefully wheeled the cart out.

"Here's our first stop," said Grandma. "The patient's name is Mrs. Jones. Let's go in."

"Hello, Mrs. Jones," said Grandma.
"This is my grandson, Herbie.
He's helping me today."

"Thank you for coming by to cheer me up!" said Mrs. Jones.

Herbie and Grandma went back to the cart.

"She's so nice," said Herbie. "I hope she isn't in the hospital for long."

"Me, too," said Grandma.

"Our next delivery is right down the hall," said Grandma.

24

"The patient's name is Mr. Maddox."
Herbie could not believe his ears.

"Lee Maddox, the Wildcats basketball superstar?" asked Herbie. "He's the best!"

Grandma and Herbie went in.
There was Kevin Maddox, a friend
of Herbie's from school.

"Hi, Herbie!" said Kevin. "I'm here visiting my Uncle Lee."

Herbie and Kevin told each other some jokes.
They laughed and laughed.

As Grandma and Herbie headed home,
Grandma said, "I hope you had fun today."

"I sure did!" said Herbie. "I made new friends and learned some new jokes. Helping at the hospital is the best!" Grandma Bear just smiled.